Merry

Happy Reading!
Uncle Bob &
Auntie Jae

Skipper's New Red Pants

by Yoko Imoto

American text by Margo Lundell

GROSSET & DUNLAP • *New York*

Originally published as SUTEKINA ZUBON by Yoko Imoto.
American translation rights arranged with KIN-NO-HOSHI CO., LTD.,
Tokyo through Japan Foreign-Rights Centre. First published in the U.S.A. in 1989 by Grosset & Dunlap, Inc., a member of
The Putnam Publishing Group, New York. Published simultaneously in Canada. Printed in Hong Kong.
Library of Congress Catalog Card Number: 88-81250 ISBN 0-448-09291-3
A B C D E F G H I J

Skipper Kitten's mother is knitting a pair of little red pants. *Click clack, click clack* go her knitting needles.

"May I put on my new pants now?" asks Skipper.

"Not until they're finished," says Mom.

Skipper holds the ball of red yarn while his mother knits. "When will they be finished?" he asks.

"Just be patient, Skipper!" says Mom.

Later that day, Skipper finds his new red pants lying on the chair. "Oh!" he cries. "They're finished!" He slips out of his yellow overalls...

And puts on his new red pants! Skipper is so happy he does a little dance.

Skipper doesn't notice that something is wrong. He thinks his new red pants look just fine!

"I can't wait to show everyone," says Skipper. And off he runs as fast as he can—with a string of red yarn trailing behind him!

First Skipper meets Mrs. Raccoon, out for a stroll with her five babies.

"See my new red pants!" he calls. "My mother made them for me."

"Oooh, pretty!" squeaks one of the babies. He doesn't notice the string of red yarn trailing behind Skipper...

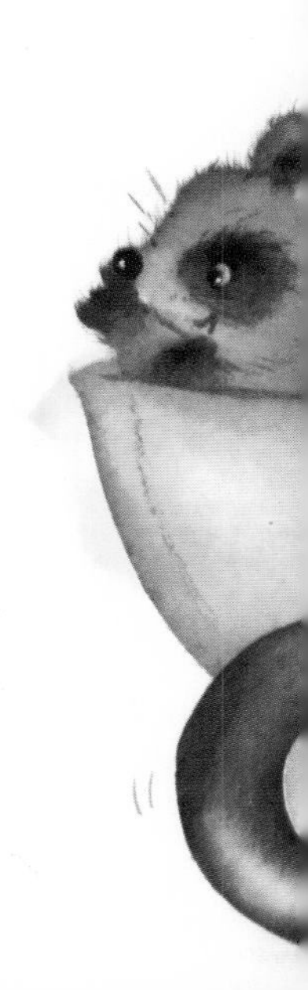

But Mrs. Raccoon does!

Next Skipper meets Betsy Bunny and her mother. He wants them to see how nice he looks in his new red pants. Skipper doesn't notice that one pant leg is getting shorter . . .

But Betsy does!

Next Skipper sees Bobby Fox coming home from baseball practice.

"Bobby will like my new red pants," thinks Skipper. He skips along happily. He doesn't notice that his pants are getting shorter and shorter...

But Bobby does!

When Skipper sees Tricia Pig, he holds his head high and marches proudly down the street. Surely Tricia will say how nice he looks in his new red pants.

Skipper doesn't notice that his pants are almost gone!

But his friends do!

When John Dog comes roller-skating by, Skipper thinks, "John will say something nice about my new red pants!"

John doesn't know *what* to say . . .

But Mike Mouse does!

"Skipper!" he cries. "You're not wearing any pants!"

"Great Cats!" says Skipper. "What happened to my new pants?"

"Were they made of red yarn?" asks Mike.

Skipper nods.

"They must have come unraveled," says Mike.

"Come on, Skipper," Mike says. "Let's wind up all the yarn and take it to your mother. Maybe she will make another pair of pants for you."

Skipper feels a little silly. His cheeks are almost as red as the yarn!

"Don't worry, Skipper," says Tricia Pig. "We'll all help."

And so they do.

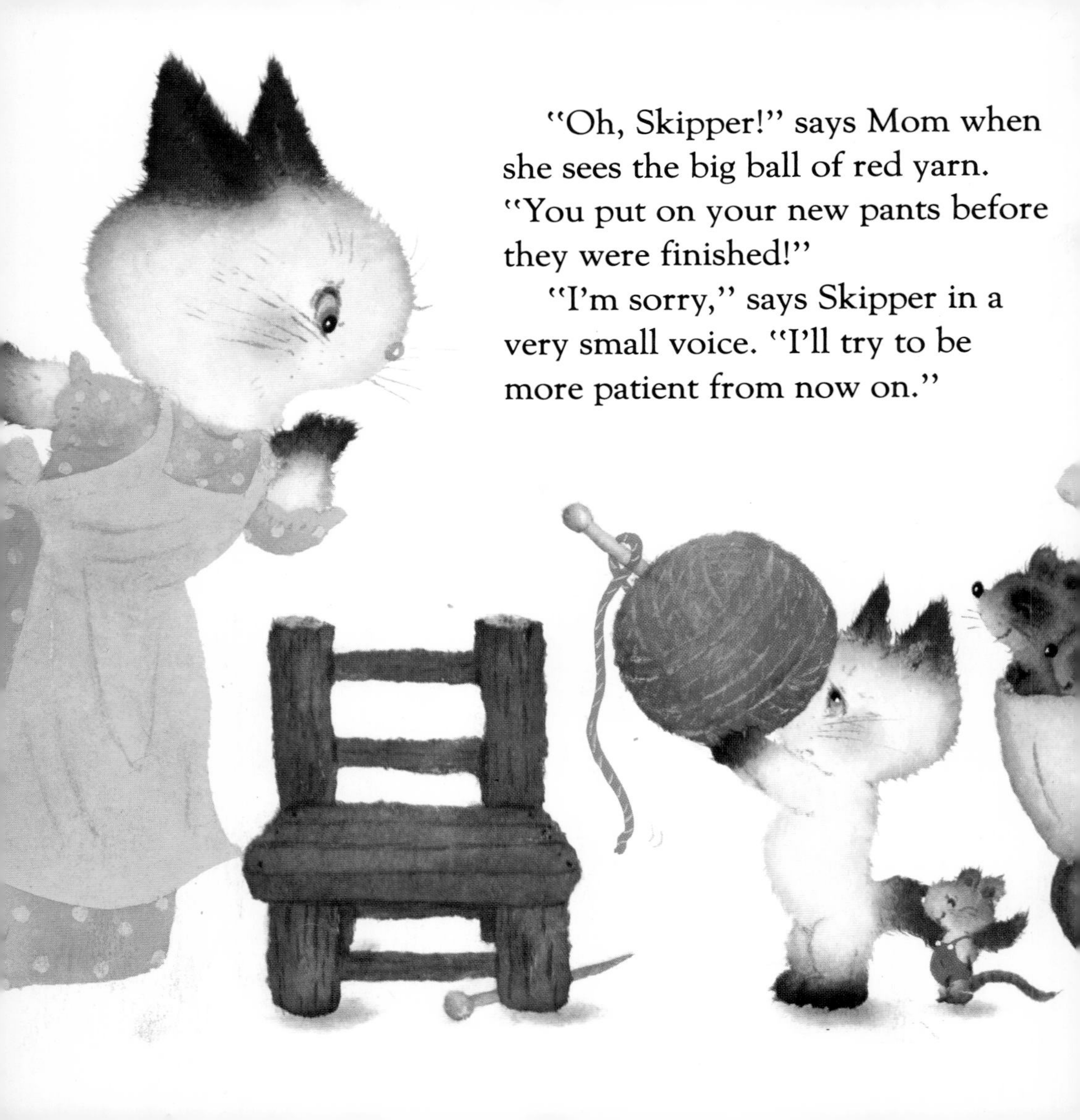

"Oh, Skipper!" says Mom when she sees the big ball of red yarn. "You put on your new pants before they were finished!"

"I'm sorry," says Skipper in a very small voice. "I'll try to be more patient from now on."